Copyright © 2023 by Emma Lee-Johnson

All rights reserved.

No part of this publication may be reproduced, distributed, or transmitted in any form or by any means, including photocopying, recording, or other electronic or mechanical methods, without the prior written permission of the publisher, except as permitted by U.S. copyright law. For permission requests, contact [include publisher/author contact info].

The story, all names, characters, and incidents portrayed in this production are fictitious. No identification with actual persons (living or deceased), places, buildings, and products is intended or should be inferred.

Book Cover by GetCovers

Edited by Stephanie Cosgrove

To, Mia,
It was lovely to connect with you
Love, Emma P ♡ for you xx

To The 97, their family members and friends.

You have been in my thoughts all these years.

Rest easy, Kopites!

You'll Never Walk Alone

A NOVELLA

SUBSTITUTION *Christmas*

EMMA LEE-JOHNSON

Synopsis

When my only blood relative makes her own plans for Christmas, the only logical thing left to do is to celebrate with my chosen family:

My fake fiancé, the billionaire owner of the football club I work for, who I am enjoying a passionate affair with.

His brother, the star striker for the same football team, who put my job in jeopardy in the first place.

Their friends, who come with a side order of complicated.

My best friends, who are all tangled up in a mess worse than your granny's oldest string of Christmas lights.

What could go wrong? With sleeping arrangements, seating plans and a massive family dinner planned, it's not going to take much to derail this Substitution Christmas.

SUBSTITUTION Christmas
A NOVELLA
Suggested Playlist

1. **Fairytale of New York**
Kirsty Mccoll and The Pogues
2. **Driving Home for Christmas**
Chris Rhea
3. **Big Spender**
Shirley Bassey
4. **Blue Christmas**
Elvis Pressley
5 **Last Christmas**.
WHAM
6. **White Christmas**
Bing Crosbie
7. **You'll Never Walk Alone**
Gerry & the Pacemakers

Contents

1. Chapter One — 1
Football Club Owner — 13
2. Chapter Two — 15
3. Chapter Three — 23
4. Chapter Four — 31
5. Chapter Five — 39
Football Strip — 47
6. Chapter Six — 49
7. Chapter Seven — 57
8. Chapter Eight — 61
Christmas Crackers — 73
9. Chapter Nine — 75
About the Author — 85
Steamy Sports Romance — 89

Chapter 1

~ Nate ~

Leila looks like my kidnap victim as we pull up into the car dealership. It's the day before Christmas Eve, and I want her present to be a surprise. Ever since she moved in with me, she has been driving one of my cars or relying on my driver or one of the security team to take her where she needs to go. That is about to change, and I hope she'll be happy with my choice. At my insistence, she has my tie wrapped around her eyes so she doesn't know where we are going.

"Are we nearly there yet, Nate? I'm feeling car sick because I can't see," she tells me.

"We are here, darling," I reply to her as I stop in the parking lot. "Just a couple more minutes and I'll take off the blindfold." As fast as I can, I park the car and run around to help her out. Having seen us arrive, the showroom manager comes out to greet us.

"Mr Cardal, come through this way." He invites me, and so I guide Leila into the spacious forecourt.

"What's that smell?" Leila whispers to me. The smell of new cars, oil, petrol and rubber all mingle creating a soup of twisted metal and high speeds.

"Don't you recognise it?" I ask her; surely, she remembers it from when she bought her pride and joy, her little yellow beetle. We had to garage her car when news of our engagement broke and the press tried to follow her every move.

Leila shakes her head at me, as we finally stop in front of my Christmas gift to her. A brand-new car. In a complete contrast to her girly, canary yellow bug-shaped car, complete with a sunflower on her dashboard, I bought her a Range Rover: a big, black, solid car that will keep her safe and give her a little privacy too. It is a top spec custom design. Now, I'm here, ready to present it to her, and I'm nervous. What if she doesn't like it? What if it's too masculine and practical?

"Are you ready?" I ask her, ignoring the nerves that bubble up in my chest. I lean up, pull the tie loose and allow it to fall freely to the ground. Leila grips her eyes closed. "Go on, you can open them now," I murmur to her, watching her reaction as she opens her big blue eyes for me.

"This is for me? You bought me a car? Oh my goodness, Nate!" She starts off whispering and ends on a screech. "I can't believe you have bought me a car. You are crazy, Nathan."

Rather cheesily, I lean forward and kiss her before whispering, "I'm crazy about you. Is it okay?"

"Okay? Nate, you bought me a car. A fricken car!" she shouts to me as she jogs around the car, looking at it from all directions. "Oh my word, Claire is going to be green with envy. She hated my Beetle almost as much as you," she tells me with a massive grin.

"I didn't hate the Beetle," I reply honestly. "It just isn't practical, especially now the media are following you everywhere!"

"You hated it; I remember what you said when you saw it: 'for fuck's sake, Leila. You can't drive around in that!'" She wobbles her head and impersonates my voice, and I have to admit, she does a pretty good job at it. "I'll be happy to have my own car again, but, Nate, this is way too generous. I actually feel embarrassed about what I have for you now."

"I do not hate that car and I'll prove it to you later," I promise her. "The car will be dropped off at the house later on today, but I just wanted to show you in case you wanted to change anything."

A gleam comes to her eyes, a sure sign that she is up to something. "It's great. However, I think I'd prefer it in yellow." She giggles and raises her eyebrows at me. Her sense of humour is wicked.

"No, I'm trying to protect you, darling. Leave the yellow cars for off road driving." I chuckle as I reply.

"Nate, it is perfect. I don't deserve all this," she softly tells me. I know she'll feel self-conscious because she is always so self-deprecating.

"I would give you the world and more, Leila. Merry Christmas, my love."

We return to my car and drive back to our home on Sandybank. Along the way, we admire the Christmas lights and decorations. When my phone begins to ring, using the car Bluetooth system, I answer it.

"Mr Cardal. I am so sorry I cannot come to work tomorrow. My mama is sick, and I must return home to see her," Giovanni, our chef, explains. We had booked him to cook for us and all our friends. It's a massive blow to our Christmas plans, especially as there are ten people to cater for. "I'm trying to get a flight back to

Italy, but with people wanting to travel home for Christmas, there isn't much left. I am going to sleep at the airport on standby for a cancellation."

Leila touches me on my knee. "Nate. Can we help him?" she asks, her voice thick with emotion. "Is there anything we can do?"

"Giovanni, I have a private jet. Once I get back to Sandybank, I will arrange for you to fly home as soon as possible. Just get all your bags packed and be ready to go," I tell him. I will have to pull in a couple of favours with the pilot I use, especially with it being so close to Christmas, but the happiness it brings Leila will be more than worth it.

"Thank you, Mr Cardal, and you too, Leila. Thank you." The chef thanks us through his tears. In the few months since Leila moved in, the two have become very close, and I know she'll want to help him in his time of need. That is one of the reasons why I fell in love with her despite us being in a fake engagement for the length of the current football season.

Once I hang up, Leila leans over and kisses me on the cheek. "That was so sweet and generous of you, thank you." And with that sort of appreciation, I would do it a million times over to make her happy.

"We just have one problem, darling. We have eight people coming for Christmas, and neither one of us is any good in the kitchen." She laughs and waves me off.

"Mere details. I know how to roast a chicken, and Louise loves to cook and bake. We can manage between us all." She is always so positive and optimistic. With her at the helm, nothing can go wrong.

~ Leila ~

"Roasting a chicken is not the same as roasting a turkey! Are you crazy?" Louise shouts at me down the phone. Having just told her that Giovanni has to return home to Italy and that me and her will take the helm in the kitchen, she freaks out on me. Louise is a planner, a meticulous planner. She has been dating Hugo, one of Nate's best friends, since our engagement party, and I already know without asking that she will have a two-year plan for their relationship, which will ultimately result in their marriage, babies and happily ever afters or they will break up.

"Come on, Louise, you love to cook. You'll get the chance to impress Hugo with your domestic skills, and it'll be fun." I try to persuade her, but she clicks her tongue at me, already forming arguments for why we can't possibly do it. "Well, if you won't help me, I think we'll have to cancel. I can't do this all on my own."

"No, wait!" she shouts at me. "Have you asked Claire to help too?" Claire is our other best friend, and I haven't asked her yet because cooking isn't something she's ever expressed an interest in. I expect her to be the entertainment, the bearer of wine and cheese and badly sung karaoke.

"No, do you think she can help?" I ask her honestly.

"Seeing as she's the only one of us that has ever prepared a Christmas dinner, yes I do." That's when I remember, Claire grew up with just her father and assumed the lady of the house role before she started primary school. "If Claire is onboard, we have a fighting chance. If not, it looks like microwave meals all around."

"Is Claire with you?" I query hopefully; maybe Louise will ask her for me.

"Yeah, she's just in the shower. Hold up." Claire and Louise live together in a little three bedroomed apartment in Redvale City centre, right in the heart of the nightlife. It is the pulse of the city. I lived with them for a year before buying my own little house on the outskirts of town. That was before I met Nate, signed a contract to pose as his fiancée for a football season and moved into his impressive pile in the celebrity neighbourhood of Sandybank. Louise must be shouting through the bathroom door, but over the sound of the shower and Claire's rendition of 'Fairy tale of New York', she has no chance of being heard. "I'll call you back; she's signing Christmas songs again."

"Okay, I'll get Giovanni to go through all the food with me. I'm sure he is ordering some stuff in already cooked; we just have to present it."

Nate is in his office with Giovanni, going over the details of where he needs to go so he can make the appropriate arrangements. Giovanni will be thankful for me rescuing him.

After knocking on Nate's office door, I walk in, and as I expected, I find Nate engrossed in his phone, trying to make the arrangements. "Hold on, Leila just walked in. Is everything okay, darling?" he asks me, winking at me when he does. Sitting in his high-backed oxblood leather desk chair, he looks even more distinguished than usual. If Giovanni wasn't sitting here, terrified that his mother might die before he can get to her, I'd probably tell Nate exactly what I am thinking.

"Am I okay to borrow Giovanni for ten minutes? I just want to go over the food plans with him so I don't mess up." Giovanni stands up gratefully, and Nate waves us out.

"Thank you, Leila. I was so nervous sitting with just Mr Cardal. He shouted at people who said no to him," Giovanni tells me in his heavily affected accent.

"Do you really think he can help me get home?" he asks, his anxiety evident in his lovely brown eyes.

"If it can be done, Nate is the person who can do it. I know he'll move heaven and earth to help you. Try to not worry too much." He hugs me and thanks me again.

"I know you always tell me that Mr Cardal is a kind man, but today I saw it like you see it. He asked me if my boyfriend can come with me to support me. My mother can meet him for the first time if he can get time off his work too. Mr Cardal said it is no extra trouble. It is very kind of him." I hug Giovanni again. I know his mother meeting his current partner is important to him, and I'm glad that with Nate's help and contacts, Giovanni will get the chance to do it.

We quickly go through the file Giovanni has collated with everything documented. It's a little overwhelming, because I have been focussed on the Christmas dinner, but I hadn't countered that anyone would need to eat for the rest of the time, which is naïve of me seeing as I have to eat every three to four hours or I become a hangry diva.

"This is pre-prepared. This is buffet food that will be displayed for you. This is what you have to make. I have all the instructions. You can do this, Leila. Just don't let Mr Cardal into the kitchen at all," he instructs me, and we share a giggle. Nate is a disaster in the kitchen; he has a knack of burning anything and everything to a crisp.

"I promise, I will keep him away," I tell him faithfully. "Claire and Lousie are going to help me," I add, hoping this will reassure him that he will have a kitchen to come back to.

"Claire is coming? And Tyson too?" Giovanni raises his eyebrows. It's no secret that Claire and Jack's best friend, Tyson, have unfinished business. It was all over the newspapers and is still gossiped about. I know Claire feels really badly about what happened, and I hope this will be an opportunity for them to clear the air.

"Everything will be fine. Tyson doesn't want to spend the day alone, and honestly, once Claire apologises and explains how things were blown out of proportion, they'll be friends again."

I only hope for all our sakes that I am right.

~ Jack ~

My friends have got to be kidding me. Sancho, a friend I met a few years ago, was supposed to be celebrating Christmas with me and my family. However, he called yesterday to tell me he has booked a last-minute trip to Jamaica to see his own family. Now, Tyson, my fellow teammate at Redvale City Football Club, is trying to bail too.

"I just think it might be a bit awkward with Claire being there. I haven't seen her since I kicked her out." Tyson and Claire hooked up at Nate and Leila's engagement party. It didn't end well when Claire was quoted in the press as calling Tyson a Cotton Candy Man and describing sex with him as similar to 'being fucked by a feather duster'. Tyson is putting up a front, but I know from his drunken rants that he genuinely felt a connection with Claire and her betrayal cut him deep.

"Maybe this is the ideal time to get your closure. You can clear the air, and both of you can move on from this mess," I suggest to him, like I have a clue with any of this crap. "Come on, you can't spend Christmas alone, and Leila will be annoyed at me if I cancel another friend. Don't leave me alone with all these people, man!" I beg him. In between the smug couples and Tyson's castoff, it's going to be lonely for me this year.

"Okay, okay. I'll come. But if it gets super awkward, I expect you to protect me." He yields.

"Of course, I will. I've always got your back. You don't need to feel awkward, though. She was the one in the wrong. If this was the other way around, you would have been dragged over hot coals. You are the one who deserves an apology." I'm not even posturing. What Claire did was harsh, and it has affected Tyson on a deep level. He was humiliated, but worse than that, he really liked her and she made a mockery of him.

"That would be hard though, seeing as I blocked her and told Redvale Public Relations to deny her any access." Well, there is that, but I'm with Tyson on this. What Claire did was wrong, and he needed to protect himself. "The mad thing is, I haven't hooked up with anyone since. Women have literally thrown themselves at me and I've denied them. She's under my skin, man!"

He'll never admit it, but Tyson has it bad. Now I understand why women like a bad boy, and the saying, 'treat them mean, keep 'em keen'. The heart wants what it wants, and recently, I have fallen victim to that myself. Ever since Nathan and Leila's engagement party, I've become restless in my own life. I want to find a special someone for myself, but having spent my whole adult life slagging about, I now find myself inadequate, unable to initiate an intimate relationship, or find a person I want that relationship with.

"Once we hit the winter break in a week's time, we'll make up for it." I promise Tyson; perhaps we could both do with blowing off some steam. So what if I haven't found 'the one' yet. Nathan waited until his mid-thirties for Leila to turn up. I'm not a monk. We both need to remember how to have fun.

With Tyson now agreeing to still come to my family Christmas, all I have left to do is buy presents for everyone. I've left it too late to use my personal shopper, and the jeweller would never have something ready in time. Christmas eve is tomorrow, and because of the way our matches have worked out, we are having our Christmas dinner tomorrow evening. I need presents and I need them now.

Wearing glasses and a hat, and borrowing one of Nathan's bodyguards, I take the risk of shopping at Marquise, a luxury retailer in fashion, beauty, and gifts. I'll be able to buy something for everyone there. Outside of London, it is the most notable shopping experience. I jot down a list of people I have to buy for plus an idea of what to buy:

Nathan *golf gloves and hat*
Leila *matching jumpers with missy*
Tyson *shirt*
Giovanni *bag*
Mrs Claybourne *smellies*
Baxter *whiskey*

Token gift: *experiences vouchers (F1 driving experience, hot air balloon, canal boat)*
  Otis, Liam, Hugo, Claire, Louise

Toys for sick children

Jameson, Nathan's bodyguard, is a strong, silent type. We shop together, him holding items while I check out other stuff. I change my mind on Mrs Claybourne's present and buy her a luxurious towelling robe and a set of mugs for her and her husband. I manage to get Giovanni a bag he has been practically fainting over. In fact, I manage to buy most of my presents before anyone recognises me; however, when they do, I am swamped instantly. Being the star striker at Redvale City football club comes with its downfalls, and unfortunately, being recognised is one of them.

Before I know what is happening, people are thanking the management for arranging for Jack Cardal to greet the children, like this was an organised event. As per my public duty, I sign some autographs, and pose for a few selfies, then allow Jameson to intervene and escort me back to the car after paying for my goods first of course.

"Did you manage to get everything you needed, sir?" Jameson asks me once we are safely back in his car.

"I wanted to get chocolate and treats for the kids at the hospital," I tell him, disappointed that I hadn't managed to get everything I wanted.

"I can go back in and buy whatever I can while you wait in the car," he offers, and as much as I wanted to pick out stuff myself, I appreciate his help.

"Yes, please. If you don't mind. If you see anything football related, I would appreciate it, Jameson, and as much as you can carry." I give him the platinum credit card I allow my staff to use. The people in Marquise will know that Jameson is helping someone influential and will offer assistance when able just by him showing that card.

While I'm in the car, I check my messages and social media. I'm just about to put my phone away when a message pings from Alana, a soap actress I've hooked up with a couple of times.

> **Are you free? Come over to mine.**

At one point I considered making things more official between us, but the lack of chemistry between us and my obvious lack of interest beyond the bedroom stopped me. Maybe I was too hasty.

> **Yeah, okay, see you soon.**

Around forty minutes later, Jameson returns with two shop assistants helping him. They have boxes and boxes of treats as well as a few bags too. This is going to be one awesome Christmas.

"Jameson, can you drop me off at the docks, please, and take these bags home for me."

Role of Football Club Owner

- Provide capital to the club and employ others (CEO, CFO etc) to deal with things such as the appointment of managers and coaching staff.
- Provide a club with a philosophical direction or ethos, a mission statement or business aim
- Control the purse strings of the club and determine the destiny of a club by the amount of investment he makes and the financial management of his club.
- Have a passion for the sport and the industry as a business.

(SOURCE: Top Soccer Blogs)

Chapter 2

~ Nate ~

After arranging Giovanni's flight back to Italy, I'm needed at the garage because Leila's new car is being delivered. "Darling, will you come with me? I want to show you something." Leila sits on the floor in the lounge, wrapping up our joint presents. With the fire roaring in the background and the Christmas tree glittering and flickering next to her, she looks like a picture-perfect wife, and my chest fills with warm pride at the very thought.

Leila insisted on wrapping the presents herself, even though Mrs Clayborne offered to do it. She said it was part of the Christmas experience. I never saw it that way, to me it was a chore, but seeing her joy, the excitement of wrapping up her presents and discussing how each person will react to them changes my mind.

"Only if you promise to make me a hot chocolate when we come back in," she demands of me. "I'm so happy Giovanni taught you how to use the machine."

"I promise to make you hot chocolate. Now come here."

After sticking a bow to the gift she has just finished wrapping, she stands up. Before I can grab her hand, she picks up our puppy, Missy, to bring with us.

"Oh no! Little Miss can wait here. We won't be long, I promise." I don't know who whines more, Leila or the dog, but it's cute either way. I lift Missy from her arms and place her gently inside her crate. We learned the hard way that Missy cannot be left alone with Christmas decorations.

"Where exactly are you taking me?" Leila asks me, so I take her by the hand to direct her and tell her at the same time.

"The big garage," I reply, knowing she hasn't been in there yet. "Your car was delivered about half an hour ago, so I had to move your Beetle into the big garage to make room for it in the little garage." The little garage is attached to the house and has enough space for eight cars. The big garage is a converted barn which is a short walk away from the main house. It's where I 'tinker' with my classic cars, or store ones I like to look at but never drive. There is something I want to show Leila.

"I can't believe everyone is going to be arriving tomorrow. It feels like we've been planning this for the longest time, and yet it appeared out of nowhere," she tells me as we walk together. "I'm really looking forward to it, despite all the last-minute hitches." She is taking everything in her stride. Last minute cancellations, staff changes, more duties. She has done herself proud. And me too. "I'm sort of dreading going to the hospital in the morning, but I really want to do it too."

Every year Redvale City Football Club visits the local children's hospital at Christmastime, bringing toys and cheer to the sickest children. It's not a nice prospect, seeing little ones so poorly they have to spend Christmas in hospital, but seeing their faces light up when they get to see their favourite footballer, or get their casts signed, or get a shirt that is signed by the whole team makes it all worthwhile. This year, Leila and I are representing the board. I know she has spent hours collecting thoughtful gifts for the sick children and their families, and also for the staff that will work throughout the festive season.

"It's heart breaking, but hopefully, we can help ease their burden and brighten up the dark times for them." I remind her, and she nods before cuddling closer to me. "So, I have brought you here to prove a point to you."

"What point? It's cold out here, Nate, couldn't you have proved your point back at the house?" I chuckle at her as I bring her into the big garage and close the door shut behind us.

"Nope, you wouldn't have believed me. You said I hated your car, but you're so wrong." She looks at me expectantly, still unaware of why I brought her out here. "How could I hate it when I own an original?"

After a short frown, she looks up at me. "So, you have a Beetle?" she asks curiously. I stop her when we arrive at the covered car that sits next to her yellow Beetle.

"Not just a Beetle. A vintage yellow Beetle," I announce as I lift the cover off the car. Her mouth opens and then closes, and she ogles the car before looking at me. "We have similar tastes."

"You could have told me this back then, Nate. This is awesome. I sincerely thought you hated my car!" Her voice becomes a little shrill as she walks around the car. My car is lighter in colour than hers, a more mellow yellow, and it has all the original features, but there is no denying that they are from the same blueprint.

"Do you believe me now? That I don't hate your car? It just wasn't safe for you to keep driving it when the press was hounding you." Now, despite our best efforts, Leila is just too high profile to drive a car like that. The more we tried to maintain her privacy, the more she became an icon to the common people. They resonated with her and now she is their idol.

"It looks like I owe you an apology, Mr Cardal," she decrees, and she walks towards me. "Do you have cameras covering this place?" I nod to her. We have security cameras everywhere. "Can you turn them off for twenty minutes? For me?"

Taking out my phone to do as she asks me, I notice a text message off Jack.

> Staying out will be back at 7am

"Jack's not coming home tonight, so we have the house to ourselves." I turn off the cameras and show her they are now not recording in the garage. "The cameras are off, darling. I'm all yours."

"Good. Get your kit off and get in that car; let's see which one is the better ride!"

Wasting no time in pulling off my sweater and kicking my shoes to one side, my trousers tighten uncomfortably when Leila follows suit. "Front or back?" I ask her, referring to the car; however, she raises her eyebrows at me, letting me know that Christmas has come early and that we are celebrating it in the best style.

"Both," she replies. She tugs her jeans down, revealing a black lacy thong that matches her balconette bra. I'll never become accustomed to how goddamn sexy she is. Curvy, yet lean. Toned but with a softness that I want to sink into. She is full in all the right places: tits, ass, and strong thighs. I couldn't have dreamed up anything more perfect. "Are you going to stand there gawking or finish what you've started?" she challenges me, pointing to my trousers that I've undone. I must have lost all train of thought when I saw her undress. She takes mercy on me and lowers them.

"You're so beautiful," I tell her honestly. I'm so glad we are spending Christmas together. We may have a temporary arrangement, but despite myself, I have fallen hopelessly in love with Leila. She forbids me from asking about the future, about the time beyond our contract, but my hope is she'll enjoy this Christmas so much that she'll know she never wants to spend it with anyone else, ever again.

"And you are so hard and big for me. God, I've missed you." It's been a couple of days since we've had sex. Leila had to travel with the team again and these are the only few days off that we have until the match on Boxing Day. "If you sit in the passenger seat, I'll sit on you." She directs me, and I can tell from her eagerness and impatience that she certainly has missed me. I lean into the car and lift the lever, pushing the seat all the way back and reclining it slightly too.

When I stand back up, she's right beside me. I pull her into my embrace and kiss her, tugging on her bottom lip. "You taste like Christmas. What have you been drinking?"

"Mulled wine. Giovanni was showing me how to warm and spice it correctly." She tastes of cinnamon and ginger, and sweetness.

Unable to resist kissing her again, I pull her close to my chest and kiss down to her neck, removing her bra so I can feel all of her against me. "Tell me. Did you use your toys while you were away?" I ask her every time she is away from me, and she tells me in detail about every time she does.

"I forgot them, Nate. I tried using my hands, but I couldn't. I was so desperate for you." As soon as I sit in the passenger seat, she climbs on top of me, writhing against me.

"Only me?" I need her to affirm it, to know that when she was frustrated and in need I was the one she thought of.

"Only you, Nate. All I want is you." I yank her thong to one side and allow her to slide down my cock, stroking the very length of me deep inside her. She exhales and throws her head back. Her pussy is already wet, and she caresses and squeezes me with every movement, her tightness enveloping me. I thrust up to meet her, neither one of us will last long at this pace. "Nate!" she calls out, letting me know that she is getting close but she needs help. I slip my hand down between our bodies, reaching for her clit, rubbing circles over it using her building wetness to ease my movements. The first tremors of her release fill me with victory, and her movements become jagged and harsh, and match her breathing.

"Come for me, Leila. All for me," I whisper to her, while her slickness coats me, pushing me over the edge. "Fuck!" I shout as I pour myself inside her, unable to hold back any longer.

"There is definitely more room in your Beetle, but I don't think your seats are as comfortable as mine," Leila murmurs to me. Her breathing is still uneven, and the most adorable blush covers her cheeks. "I'm not finished with you yet, Nate. This might be our only chance to make love under the Christmas tree." My body, sated only seconds ago, already throbs for more of her promised adventure.

"I've not had my fill of you yet either, baby. That was just a tension breaker," I tell her, causing her to laugh. "Did I surprise you?" She frowns in confusion, so I spread my hands. "With my taste in cars!"

She laughs again. "You did, but it was a nice surprise. Maybe one day, we can both take our yellow cars out for a drive."

"You'll have a hard job. There's no engine in this one," I tell her.

"Aww, baby! Is it old and decrepit like you?" She teases me. I'm ten years older but, as the saying goes, 'you're only as old as the woman you feel'. I've never felt in better shape. "Don't worry, I'll look after you."

"Don't be so cheeky. I'm not over the hill just yet, and I'll prove it tonight. I hope you've slept well, Leila, because there won't be time for sleeping tonight. I'm going to fuck you all night long."

"Is that a threat... or a promise?" she queries me sassily.

"No, darling. That's a guarantee."

CHAPTER 3

~ Leila ~

Seeing Nate's yellow Beetle reminds me that we do have a lot in common despite our different beginnings. I keep seeing the reasons why I won't fit into his world once the contract is over, but everyday brings new evidence of why we belong together. Maybe that is foolish of me, naïve even. But it's going to crush me when we are over, so I may as well enjoy what we have right here, right now. Loving Nate is the easy part. Him finding out about it and not feeling it back is the dangerous part. However, it's Christmastime, and if we can't get carried away now, when can we?

After using the bathroom in the big garage, we return back to the house. It's the first time I've had a free rein to decorate somewhere other than my little house. With the help of our Christmas task force, I made Nate's vast home into a winter wonderland. Even Jack appreciates it, and he is verging on being a grinch. With the boughs of holly, festive lights, the large, tastefully decorated Christmas trees, and the full-sized, hand carved nativity scene, it is a faux North Pole paradise outside Nate's house.

Inside, the house is just as pretty with wreaths up the double staircase, Christmas trees in most of the rooms and scenes set up for enticing mood and perfect photo opportunities. We even have a hot chocolate bar set up for our guests. Nate smiles at me, humouring me as I indulge in every fad I've ever dreamed of.

Missy sleeps in her crate. She's still only a puppy, so while she needs her walks and play time, she also needs lots of naps. Nate sits down in front of the fire and pats the ground beside him, inviting me over too. The natural warm light from the fire gives him an ethereal glow.

"Thank you," I whisper to him, a lump forming in my throat from sheer happiness. "This has been by far the best start to Christmas I've ever had. I'm really looking forward to the rest of it." Before I can look away, he catches my chin and forces me to look at him.

"Are you crying?" he asks me, alarm and confusion dripping from his tone and stance.

"Not crying. I've never felt as happy as I do right now. At this exact moment, I simply feel grateful and extremely lucky that Jack fucked my life up like he did. Otherwise, we wouldn't be having this perfect Christmas together." I laugh a little. I didn't think I'd ever get to the point when I'd be thankful for Jack for almost destroying my career.

Nate wipes away a fallen tear with his thumb. "I've never felt as happy either. You did all this, Leila. You made Christmas happen. You've made me so happy. I want every Christmas to be like this one." I clam up; I don't want to talk about beyond our contract. If this is all it is meant to be, that's okay. But I don't want to mar what we have by muddying the waters.

"I'm sure they will be. Are you sure Jack isn't coming home?" I ask, changing the subject.

"No, he isn't, Mrs Claus," he replies, pulling me flush with his chest. "It's just you and me. All night long."

Even though we've only just finished, arousal swirls around my tummy; I need him. I don't think I'll ever stop needing him. So, while he is mine, I'm taking everything I can get. "Just how I like it. So, I've apologised for saying you hated my car. Now it's time to thank you for my car." I'm about to straddle him once more when he flips me over, landing between my legs.

"Oh no, now it's my turn to show you how sorry I am for making you doubt me." He presses against me; he is hard again and that delights me. "I want to make you forget you ever thought it, so I'm going to replace it with an even better memory."

He undresses me, kissing every inch of my skin, and tells me to lie still. He leaves the room and then returns a minute later with food in his hands. I spot the spray cream first, then the strawberries and the chocolate dip. It looks like Nate is going to feed me, though why I have to be naked is news to me.

The can of spray cream is cool against my skin. Nate rolls it over my tummy and down my left thigh before he shakes it and squirts the cream onto my nipples. They pucker and stand to attention against the cold, light cream that sits upon them. Nate uses his tongue to mop up the mess, trailing it lazily over my entire breast, spreading the cream further, then he switches to my other breast. The sensations flow through me when something else is added to the mix, something a bit rougher, and more rounded.

A strawberry.

Nate uses it to tease me. First across my nipples then down between my legs. "Where shall I touch?" he whispers against my provoked skin, and a shiver of delight chases down my spine at his hushed words. He teases me further, completely missing my pussy and trailing the juicy fruit down my inner thigh. "Just here?" he asks with a smirk as I writhe against him.

"No. You know where I want it!" I tell him, even though I know he won't do it until I practically spell it out to him. "I want you to rub it along my pussy, first on my clit, but then I want you to fuck me with it. Then after I come on it, I want you to eat it."

"You've got such a filthy mind, darling. I fucking love it," he tells me, and finally, he gives me what I want. "Is this what my dirty girl wants?" he asks me as he gently glides the strawberry through my lips and over my clit.

"Harder!" I gasp, my whole-body pulsing in reaction. I'm proud to be his naughty, filthy girl. He makes it so easy to let all my inhibitions go, to demand and take everything I want. "Nate, I want you."

"Beg me." he tells me sternly.

"Please!" I shout at him, already moving to all fours so he can fuck me hard and deep.

"Please what?" He teases, even as he presses his hard cock at my entrance.

"Please fuck me. Fuck me hard. NOW!"

He gives me everything I want and more, thrusting into me in one swift move until he is fully seated inside me.

The tremors of my release start almost immediately. Nate, as accommodating as ever, thrusts deep and hard from behind, while still rubbing the strawberry over my clit. The intensity blinds me of all reason; I am just a pulsing orgasm. The fulfilment is all embracing, and I never want it to end.

"Come on, gorgeous. Have you got one more for me?" Nate asks me gruffly as he continues to pound at me. I'm about to tell him that I don't, that I'm done, when I feel the seeded exterior of the strawberry once again; maybe it's the same one, maybe it's a fresh one, but Nate's arm is no longer around my waist. His hands are on my ass. While he thrusts his cock into my pussy, stroking me deep inside, he uses the strawberry to tease my back entrance too. "This will be mine soon enough too, Leila. Promise?"

"I promise. I'm not going to last much longer, Nate." I warn him. Every inch of me shakes, and I think I'm going to collapse from all the thrills he has given me.

"Then come for me; we'll come together." He slaps my ass and pushes me to the limit of my restraint. I call out his name as I come for the third time and bury my face into the rug in front of the fire when my arms give out on me. My whole body could be a massive puddle. Fluid filled without any power or definition. Nate is still filling me with his load when I gasp for air. I don't think either one of us will last all night long.

"Holy shit. It just gets better every time" I say to him when he pulls out of me. We clean up each other, kissing and teasing one another while we do. He throws a t-shirt to me that I pull on before telling him I need the toilet.

"Wait, I'll come up with you. I've still got something to show you that I won't be able to do when our friends get here." Nate is always so very generous. Not a day goes by when he doesn't surprise me with something that I know he has put thought into it. It might be a KitKat when he knows I'm due on my period and need a chocolate fix, or a new collar for Missy but he is always thinking of me and of us.

"You got me another present?" I guess; however, he nods his head then shakes it.

"In theory, yes. But I think this is going to be as much for my pleasure as it is for yours." Suitably intrigued, I dash up the stairs, with Nate closely following me. "You'll have to give me a couple of minutes. I put it away safe so Mrs Claybourne didn't find it."

"It's something naughty, isn't it?" I shout as I laugh.

"I'm not telling you; go and have your wee, and I'll be ready when you've finished," he tells me sternly.

"But I was going to have a shower too. Don't you want to jump in with me?"

"Goodness, woman! You're going to be the death of me!" he exclaims; however, he follows me into the bathroom and begins running the shower while I use the toilet. "I suppose we can clean up now, ready for round two in a couple of hours," he says as he winks at me.

Before joining him in the shower, I grab two towels and place them on the side for us when we are finished. When I step under the rainfall shower, I sigh in reaction. My entire body still hums in satisfaction, and the promise of more later is enough to turn my tummy to lava again.

We tend to share a shower a lot, and we therefore have our own routine worked out. Nate will wash my hair, while I always insist on us both using an exfoliator. I always scrub his back for him because he enjoys the roughness of it. Nate always ensures we are properly rinsed off, though I believe this may be so he gets to touch me all over. He's been known to add suds to areas he wants to examine more thoroughly, mostly my breasts and between my legs. Most of the time we end up needing another shower because we can't keep our hands off each other.

When we are both done, I step out first and hand him a towel before picking up my own. "Can I dry your hair? I don't want you catching a cold." No matter how much I try to reassure him that you cannot catch a cold that way, he still insists on drying my hair, and it's nice that he wants to take care of me, and so I always let him.

After drying and moisturising, I tug on my Christmas pyjamas to match the duvet cover on our bed. Nate thought Christmas bedding was not a thing! So, I insisted that every bed had its own set. Now, I think he likes it just as much as me.

"So, are you going to show me my surprise now?" I ask him, noticing that he is wearing the Christmas pyjamas I ordered for him too. Nate looks down on me adorably. I know from that expression that he's feeling a little self-conscious. "Please... I'm sure it's amazing. And it'll make me feel better about the present I have for you too."

"Okay, you win. But I want to blindfold you again. It was kinda hot when we did that today, wasn't it?" I nod to him, having my sight restricted seemed to heighten every other sense. It would be wonderful to try it again. "Close your eyes for me, then."

Obediently, I do as I am asked.

Chapter 4

~ Leila ~

Nate wraps a black silky strip of material over my eyes and pulls tight, blinding me. Almost instantly, my hearing piques and the hairs on my arms stand on end. In the corner, I can hear rustling and what I think is the opening of a box. Then suddenly, I jump when something tickles my arm.

"Don't worry, darling. It's just me. I want to tease you a little and see how far we can push it. Is that okay?" he murmurs to me.

"Yes," I reply shyly, as heat already builds between my legs. The same sensation prickles my lips, a light, fluffy sensation that provokes my senses but only lightly. If my nose was uncovered, I'm sure I would sneeze. Then, the featherlight weight transfers to my neck, down over my boobs and tummy, and then down each leg, one at a time. My skin tingles where it makes contact, all of it travelling and manifesting in my tummy and down to the junction between my thighs.

"What about something a little harder? Would you like me to try that?" Nate murmurs to me, shocking me when I realise he is behind me, not in front of me like I thought. I nod to him, but he tuts at me. "Tsk. No, baby. I need to know for definite. I never want to hurt or frighten you. Use your words."

"I want to try it, Nate. I want to try everything with you," I tell him, and my honesty and forwardness are rewarded with a kiss from Nate; he turns my head to the side and kisses me deep and hard. However, he pulls away when I try to move in for more.

"Sorry, gorgeous. You know I have trouble concentrating when you're around me." He chuckles. Before I can react, something smooth and cool rolls over my cheek. It's heavier than the first item, but the different sensation only fuels my pent-up frustration. After running it over my earlobe, Nate pushes it into my mouth, it tastes metallic and is shaped like a pointed bullet… "This is brand new out of the box, and eventually, you'll walk around with this in for me, won't you, Leila?"

I nod until he pulls the item out of my mouth. "Yes. I'm looking forward to it," I tell him. We've been edging towards anal play for a little while. I've never tried it before and have never trusted anyone enough until now.

"You are such a good girl for me tonight. Can I pull off your panties and eat you?" Involuntarily, I squeeze my thighs together as the heat pools between them. How can I want him so much already? "That's my good girl. Show me how wet this has made you, and then I can show you one more thing before my final surprise."

Nate holds my hands to help me stand and then pulls down my PJ bottoms and underwear at the same time. He sniffs at me. "You're so wet and hot already; give me your hand," he demands, and I hold out my hand for him. "Feel for yourself how much you like this, baby." He pushes my hand to my pussy, and with relative ease, I slip a finger through the wetness, shivering in reaction. He's hardly touched me, and I'm a quivering knot of need. I aim my finger to graze my clit, but Nate possessively removes my hand. "No, it's mine. I want the pleasure of doing it. Do you want to stand or sit?"

Knowing as soon as Nate uses his expert tongue and fingers on me my legs will give way, I sit on the edge of the bed. Nate takes my hand again and places something against my palm. Upon further inspection, using my fingertips, I identify a stiff leather handle that transforms into lots of soft strips of leather. I've never used one, but I believe it is a flogger. Before I finish my examination, Nate's mouth connects with my clit. His tongue works it until the flogger lays forgotten in my hands. Then as soon as it starts it stops. I grope around for the flogger, but I can't find it.

"Kneel up on the bed for me, beautiful," he asks me harshly; I know this is really turning him on now. I slowly remove my top first, earning a groan from him. Then I climb on top of the bed on all fours, sashaying my hips as I do. Part of me tenses in anticipation in case Nate uses the flogger on me. I imagine it to be like a million mini whips against my skin, and I'm not entirely sure that I will like that. As always, Nate shocks me when instead of inflicting pain, he trails the flogger down my back. The tickling along my sensitive skin causes me to arch my back. "That's it, gorgeous, let me see your pussy, show me where you want me to lick."

Eager to please him, I arch my back a little more, while also pushing out my butt and spreading my legs wider. The tickling continues across my ass cheeks and down my legs. He's torturing me. "Nate!" I warn him, my hips already beginning to buck.

"Shush, beautiful," he argues back, continuing with the flogger back up to my back. Tantalising me and provoking my desires until they throw a tantrum at his goading. "I'm going to take off the blindfold and I want you to lie on your back. It's time for your reward for being a good girl."

Nate pulls on the silky, makeshift blindfold, allowing it to fall away and rolls me onto my back. "That was hot. I liked it, but I'm also really frustrated," I tell him honestly.

"You looked incredible. I adore you, and your trust in me, Leila. Now lie back, I want to see you enjoy this." Nate drags the flogger over each of my breasts. My nipples pucker in reaction to the super sweet sensation, and my skin goose pimples. It's different without the blindfold because I can see and anticipate the feelings as they develop in front of me. However, the edge of danger has gone too. "Which way is better?" he asks, tracing the contour of my tummy until he reaches my pussy again.

"Both have their advantages. I'm open to doing both again," I answer, and he grins at me and my answers.

"Good girl. Open your legs wider for me." I do as he asks, but the sensation isn't enough; I need more. I buck against the flogger that grazes over the place I desperately need more. "You need more? I don't want to hurt you." I know he is warning me that it might hurt, but I need it. I need all the sensations he can inflict on me.

"Please!" I breathily plead. "Just a little harder." Nate flicks his wrist, and although the flogger comes down a little harder, it's still not enough. "Harder, Nate. Harder," I cry out until finally the flogger connects with my pussy, biting into my sensitive skin, stinging me until all that matters is the wonder that flows through my body as he brings it down on me again. On the third strike, my body begins to splinter apart as my orgasm blows through me. My butt cheek clench and shivers run all over my body as wave after wave of pleasure wash over me.

"Wow, you've never looked more beautiful. Now, I'm gonna kiss it all better for you." Nate's warm tongue and caressing lips replace the flogger, and as the tendrils of delight begin to recede, he coaxes them back again, making my release last even longer.

With his mouth eating away at the very heat of me, I think I must have been a very good girl this year. Either that, or Santa forgot to check his list twice!

~ Nate ~

The night is going exactly as I planned, and now I'm inching towards the pinnacle. The grand finale as it will be. I only hope Leila is enjoying it as much as I am. I've never used any of this stuff before, but somehow it feels right. Just as I thought, Leila seems to really enjoy it, and that is more of a turn on for me than anything else could be.

While she is still coming, I caress her pussy with my tongue, hoping to elongate any pleasure she experiences, and from her moans and movements, I think I'm doing a pretty good job. Using the tip of my tongue, I slowly tease her clit that seems to have a pulse all of its own and revel in her pants and groans as her orgasm continues to flow through her.

She looks like an angel. A very naughty one, I'll admit, but also a very satisfied one.

"Nate, my body feels like it's full of lead. I think I need a nap after all that!" she confesses to me, and I flash a massive grin at her, happy with my work. "However, now it's your turn for a little pampering." As enticing as it sounds, I am completely satisfied and want to join her for a nap.

"Babe, I'm more than happy. I actually want to snuggle with you, but I have just one more little thing for you. Well, for us," I tell her, and although she is in a stupor, she tries to at least open her eyes and look attentive. "I wanted something for us for when you're travelling with the team and we can't be together."

"Like my Rose?" she asks, referring to her suction toy we have been relying on when she travels.

"Yes, like your Rose, but with an upgrade." This captures her full attention. "I wanted something that I could be involved in. I hope you like it."

From the side of the bed, I pull out the gift bag from Lovehoney. Her eyes immediately light up, and she sits up attentively. "That's where I got The Rose from too. It's a decent shop, isn't it?" she tells me. I sit down beside her and pull her onto my lap with the gift bag resting at my side.

"It was an eye-opening experience. Maybe next time we could go together. There is such an extensive variety that I had trouble choosing," I suggest, and despite me being fully sated and ready for a nap, my cock has a life of its own, raising its head and hardening of its own according at the mere thought of shopping with Leila for sex toys.

"I'd really like that, Nate, but what if the press saw us?" she asks, and although it's a valid question, to hell with it.

"And what? You're my fiancée and they can write what they want about our shopping hazards. It's got fuck all to do with anyone else," I tell her fiercely; she kisses me quickly and then tugs on my bottom lip. "Unless you're too shy?"

"No, I'm not shy, not with you. You're right, it's got nothing to do with the media and the public, and we have the right to shop wherever we want to."

"That's my girl... so, do you want to see what I picked out?" I ask, turning the subject back to what I wanted to discuss in the first place. She nods to me and smiles widely as she slides off my lap and releases my swollen cock from its prison. "Now, if you don't like it, we can pick something else, maybe we should have done this together?"

"Nate! Will you just show me already?" she squeaks at me, so I hand her the gift bag and let her see for herself. The model I chose is a love egg vibrator with app control.

"I thought we could video call and then have some fun. You would keep the actual toy, and I will access the app and tell it what to do in my physical absence," I explain to her as simply as I can, mostly because I don't fully understand how it works myself; it'll be something we can work out together.

"Wow. I've heard of these toys, but I never envisioned having one. I think it's cool. I can't wait to try it out," she tells me. "You've bought amazing presents, Nate. How can I ever thank you for your generosity?"

"The biggest thanks I want is to see you happy, darling. As long as you're happy, I'm a contented man. Merry Christmas, gorgeous."

"Merry Christmas, Nate. It's going to be the best Christmas ever. It already is," she tells me. We naturally fall onto the bed and spoon each other, dozing off peacefully in each other's arms until an alarm goes off. I leave Leila to sleep while I check the security camera. Sure enough it's Jack coming home early. Hell, it's barely even midnight.

"Stop the orgy, love birds," he shouts up to us while laughing at his own joke. "I couldn't be bothered with Alana, so I came home early."

"You were spending the night with Alana?" I ask him, keeping my voice down so we don't disturb Leila.

"Yeah I was, and it was all going great until she told me she wanted a threesome," he tells me grumpily. "I jumped at the chance, thinking Christmas had come early. Then in walks this big hulk of a man. I thought she meant another girl. So, I told her that wasn't my scene and came home."

Inevitably, I laugh at him and his woeful story. "I thought you were looking for 'the one'. You ruled Alana out weeks ago."

"Yeah, I know. But it's Christmas and I fancied a shag, so I said yes when she invited me to hers. I should have known she'd butcher the whole thing." I laugh at him again, and reluctantly, he eventually joins me.

"Come on, we best get some sleep. We have a big day tomorrow." Jack yawns as if on cue.

"Yep, we have to be at the hospital for 8 a.m." I remind him. "I'm going back to bed to Leila. Your night might be screwed, but mines only just beginning!"

"Uh! Gross!"

Chapter 5

~ Nate ~

We arrive at the Children's hospital with the rest of the team, coaching staff and board members, and although this is a newer building to the one I was treated at all them years ago, it still brings back memories I would rather forget.

To be required to stay in hospital over the Christmas period means that the children we will meet today are the sickest children in the country. Meeting them and their families, even if it is only for a minute or two, will give them a boost in their morale and a treat that they especially deserve.

Due to the severity of their illnesses, we are only allowed to stay for thirty minutes, which means in groups of three or four, we all attend different parts of the hospital at the same time. We each make five visits to wards, and then before we leave, we spend time outside the rooms of the children in isolation. Some aren't even allowed contact with their parents. That thought alone makes my chest tighten.

As prearranged, Leila and I team up with Jack to make our visit. We have two assistants helping us carry all the items we purchased for the children. Our first patient is a little girl called Grace who is seven years old. She has mid-length brown hair and cute little glasses and a tube that is taped to her face and snakes up her right nostril. Around her bed is a plethora of Disney princesses. I know Leila will have the perfect gifts for her. Grace's mother smiles widely at us when we walk into the room. "Look who it is, Gracie. I told you he'd come and see you!"

The barest whisper of a sweet angelic voice calls out, "Jack-the-lad!" making us all laugh with her. While Leila sits with Grace's mother and Jack talks about football with Grace, I arrange the gifts for her and her mother. Football shirts, chocolate and sweets, a doll, books, and a laptop. Leila also packed up some pamper items for the parents, knowing their self-care is probably the last thing on their minds right now.

When I return to the room, I can see Leila is moved almost to tears. She told me the previous two years have been the same for her. Grace calls out excitedly when she sees I have gifts. I give Jack the honours of giving them to her, knowing he is her hero and that it'll mean so much more to them two.

"Nate, this is Donna, Grace's mum. I've passed on our details. I'd like to keep in touch with them," she tells me, and I can see, despite her outward confident display, that she is unsure of herself.

"That's a wonderful idea, darling." I reassure her. "It was lovely meeting you, Grace. We have to visit some of the other boys and girls now. Merry Christmas, sweetheart." However, after fist bumping Jack, her attention is firmly back on her pile of presents, and rightly so.

"Bye-bye, Jack and friends. Thank you for all the stuff you brought us. Happy Christmas."

Our next visit rips my heart out. A baby, no older than six-month-old, with masses of tubes and wires attached to his body. The machines that keep him tethered to this world whirl and beep, and his broken parents stand vigil over their precious child's body. They both look at the door when we knock. Their eyes seem vacant, and I just want to hold them and tell them everything will be okay. However, I cannot guarantee that. Life is so fragile and if this experience isn't a stark reminder of that, I don't know what would be.

We speak to the parents and discover that they have three other children, who will be spending Christmas with their grandparents, and we ensure we leave enough presents for everyone, especially the siblings, who will be missing their parents and dealing with a lot of upheaval.

After visiting the other three children on our list, we go to the isolation ward. There is a long row of rooms; each one is cut off from the outside with the exception of the viewing window. As I child, I stayed in one of these rooms too, and the thought of these little ones having to do the same is devastating. The other players are also here, and they all perform a few tricks for the children, which seems to brighten their day. They communicate with us with a white board; however, their expressions tell their stories. What they've been through, what they've yet to face and the little pockets of joy such as this one that make a mountain of difference.

After leaving the hospital, Jack and Leila are quiet and sombre, just like me. "It's officially time to celebrate our Christmas," I tell them. For the next forty-eight hours we are off-duty. "I know seeing all those children, seeing how sick they are and how much they've endured is heart breaking, but carpe diem!" I shout it a little louder than I intended, but I need to break their downward spiral. "Life is short, and we should use today as an example of why we need to be grateful for every moment we have together." I look at Leila when I say the final line and share a smile with her.

"Come on, love birds. It's time to go home before you two make me puke. You are far too in love for me to be dealing with this early in the morning," Jack complains loudly, which only encourages me all the more. Pulling Leila to me, I swing her around in my arms as I kiss her and laugh when she squeals. I don't even care when the tell tale clicking and flashing of the press intrudes. Let them take pictures; I want the world to see and know how happy I am.

"Merry Christmas, gorgeous," I whisper to her. "I feel like I already got my presents," I confess to her, because with Leila in my arms, in my bed and one hundred percent in my heart and soul, all my Christmas dreams have already come true.

~ Jack ~

The hospital visits to see the children is always a humbling experience, and sharing it with Nathan and Leila only deepens the feeling of gratitude I have for the life I live, the people I share it with and the privilege I am blessed to have. Yes, my threesome went tits-up last night. Yes, I feel lonely sometimes and misunderstood. But, I have so much to be grateful for.

Listening to Leila and Nathan's conversation when we get back to Sandybank, I begin to see a way in which I can make a better difference in the lives of the children who need our support more than ever. "Donna said that she has been unable to work and now her landlord is evicting her. Grace is seriously ill; she needs a kidney transplant and has to stay on constant dialysis until a donor is found." Leila is evidently distressed by the information she managed to get from Grace's mum and rightly so. In their hour of need, they are being kicked in the teeth and that doesn't sit well with me.

"Do we have any appropriate homes they could live in?" I ask my brother. Nathan initially made his fortunes in property and technology. Between us, we retain the joint business our father founded and left to us after he died.

"I'll contact Kym now and see if she knows. It is Christmas Eve though, Jack. We might not get an immediate answer," he replies to me, already tapping away on his phone.

"Yes. It is Christmas Eve, and there is a sick little girl out there who needs us. Her mother needs our support, and I want to help. I want to stay anonymous though. This is important, Nathan!" I retort back to him.

"That's such a lovely thing to do, Jack. Thank you," Leila says to me, giving me a sense of pride in myself that I have never felt before. "I am willing to act as your conduit and say an anonymous donor reached out to me."

I nod to her, not trusting my voice to give away how emotional it all makes me feel.

"Kym says we have no properties available right now but there are three new builds available close to the hospital that we can invest in."

"Can we go and see them?" I jump up as I ask him, but he shakes his head at me.

"Sorry, no can do. I promised to help Leila with the food, remember?" My heart begins to fall in disappointment when Leila laughs out loud at my brother.

"This is perfect then, you two can go and view the properties while I crack on with the food. I do not want you in that kitchen, Nate. You're a fucking nightmare!" Leila tells us, and I involuntarily laugh out loud at my brother's expense. "What are you laughing at? You're not much better. Could you take Missy with you though, Nate? You know she'll distract me."

My brother stands, paces to his fiancée and kisses her deeply right in front of me once again. That man never seems to have his fill of his partner. "Put her down for god's sake!" I tell him in mock disgust, pretending to avoid them by getting Missy ready for our adventure. "Tyson should be here in about an hour. Look after him, please, Leila, and keep him away from Claire. He'll bolt otherwise."

Leila assures me she has everything under control as she waves us off. My brother drives us to the new estate that is currently being built. We already own a few properties here, but they are either rented out privately or through the football club for players and employees. Nathan felt it was important to offer players, particularly the ones from other countries, a temporary place to call home. This made their move here less intimidating and the transition a lot smoother. We pass the large brick entrance that bears the sign "Loughby Grange", the name of the new estate. It is all decorated with wreaths and Christmas lights, and it looks idyllic. A pleasant family dwelling.

Nathan points out a couple of the houses we already own. "This is one of ours; that is where Piotr lives now." The imposing home looks far too big for a young man and his girlfriend, but as we drive past, we can see him and his whole family celebrating the festive season.

The houses for sale are smaller than Piotr's one, but as three bedroomed detached houses, they are still more than substantial for Grace and her mum. After viewing the first one and being assured all three are identical, I tell Nathan I want to buy them.

"Are you sure you want all three? Shall we make this part of our joint portfolio?" he asks me, and I know no matter what choice I make, Nathan won't judge me or hold it against me.

"I want to buy one for Grace, but we can share the other two." Nathan nods, dials a number, and tells them we want all three.

"Come on, let's get back and tell Leila the good news. Once the contract goes through, she can call Donna and let her know," he says to me, and I know he cannot wait to get back to Leila. A few months ago, his behaviour would have knocked me sick, but now, I hope I find my special someone sometime soon.

Maybe next year I could be celebrating Christmas with my significant other too.

We return home to chaos. We can hear the shouting before the car comes to a stop outside. That doesn't sound good at all. We open the door to see Claire and Tyson facing off against each other, both looking as fired up and determined as the other.

"I'm not having this. It is Christmas. You two need to get over yourselves. Please apologise to one another and shake hands!" Leila shouts at them both.

"I'm sorry I called you a tart and threw you out of my house," Tyson stays steadily to the girl who broke his heart and made him a laughingstock.

Claire, who I know is fierce and loud, barely whispers her response. "I'm sorry I told everyone you fuck like a feather duster." I'm sure she cries as she runs away, but my concern lies with my best friend. Tyson, however, asks for a brandy and shakes his head at me.

"I knew this would be torture, Jack. You owe me big time for this!"

As if on cue, Missy cocks her leg and pees on his boots.

Football strip

A football strip is the standard equipment and attire worn by players. The minimum kit which a player must use is specified by the sport's rules, and anything that is deemed dangerous to either the player or another participant is prohibited.

The basic equipment which must be worn by all players includes a shirt (also known as a jersey), shorts, socks (also known as stockings), footwear and shin pads.

Footballers generally have their surname and identifying numbers on the backs of their shirts. For example Jack has 'Cardal' across the top and he is number 9 in the squad

(SOURCE: The Football Association)

CHAPTER 6

~ Leila ~

Once Nate and Jack leave, I crank the kitchen into action. The large Range ovens are roaring and waiting to be filled with turkey, gammon, pigs-in-blankets, vegetables, potatoes and stuffing balls. On the stove top is gravy, bread sauce and cranberry jelly. In the steamer are more fresh vegetables, primed to start when we are ready. Claire will help me with all the seasoning and timings when she arrives, which should be any minute now.

I quickly get to work on the selection of starters we have for all our guests, and once the salads and garnishes are arranged prettily in the serving bowls, I take a quick look over the sleeping arrangements that Ms Claybourne has kindly left for me in the folder we use to pass messages. I sit down with it in the main living room with the largest tree of our collection. My heart quickens when I see that the only single rooms are next door to each other. Claire and Tyson are the only single guests, but them sleeping next to each other might cause problems considering their past.

Quickly looking through the chart, I wonder if there is another room I can move one of them to, but the gate alarm beeps, signalling the arrival of my first guest. Shit!

When I reach the front door, Tyson's low and shiny sports car pulls to a stop in the temporary parking area. "Merry Christmas, Doc!" he shouts to me as she jumps out. He swiftly lifts two bags from his boot before following me inside. "Am I the first to arrive?" he asks me, looking unsure of himself.

"Yes, but don't worry. Jack and Nate will be back shortly; they just had some last-minute business to take care of," I tell as he peers into the kitchen with alarm rising in his eyes. "You can get settled in your room if you like, or I can make you a drink or something to eat."

He hands me a bag with wrapped gifts inside. "A drink would be nice, beer if you have one. Can I put these under the tree, please?" I direct him to the main living room with the biggest tree while I get his drink.

"I'll just be a minute," I tell him. When I return with his cold beer, I find him peering over the sleeping plan. "Doc, this isn't going to work. I'm going to try my best to stay out of her way, but this is going to make it so hard." He points down to the plan to the spot between his and Claire's rooms.

"Don't worry, Ms Claybourne arranged this; I was just about to swap it up." I move his sticker to Jack's spare room. They can help me move everything later. "For what it's worth, Tyson. She regrets hurting you. I know she violated you in the most horrible way, but I do think she has genuine remorse for what went down."

He nods stiffly at me, a blush covering his face. "I'd rather just forget about everything," he says bleakly. "Claire made her thoughts and feelings clear, and I was foolish to let my guard down. I've also learnt my lesson."

The gate alarm beeps again, and I stand to greet my next guest. When I see the long saloon car gliding up the driveway, I warn Tyson. "It's Claire." He quickly gets to his feet, lifting his overnight bag.

"I'll go and get settled in my room then. Tell Jack where I am when he gets home," he requests before gulping the rest of his beer. I walk him to the hallway to point him in the direction of his room.

Claire takes us both by surprise though. Wearing a Santa hat and a hideous Christmas jumper that plays music and flashing lights, she falls through the door and shouts. "Merry Christmas, motherfucker!" Her face, so bright and happy, seems to freeze in horror when she lays eyes on Tyson. Tyson shuffles uncomfortably next to me. "Oh. It's you. I thought Mr Cardal had bought Leila a flashy car." She points to Tyson's car on the front.

Involuntarily, I snort at Claire's assumption. I wouldn't be seen dead in a flashy car like Tyson's. "No, just me, Mr Candy Cane," He incorrectly air quotes Claire. Her face flushes with anger and embarrassment.

"If you're going to quote me, dickhead, do it properly. It's Cotton Candy Man, actually," she shouts at him.

It doesn't take long for the whole arrangement to dissolve into disarray.

The gate alarm beeps again, and I pray out loud for it to please be Nate. Tyson and Claire argue and shout at one another.

"I'm not having this. It is Christmas. You two need to get over yourselves. Please apologise to one another and shake hands!" I shout at them both. I wait like their hen-pecking mother until they relent.

I look pleadingly at Nate to help me, but Claire and Tyson make amends on their own accord. "Come on, guys. It's Christmas, and this means a lot to Leila.

I think we can all get along for forty-eight hours, right?" Nate says as he takes my hand.

Everyone nods and smiles superficially, but I can sense the tension already. Why did I agree to a chosen family Christmas? This is going to be a car crash!

"Jack, apparently I'm sleeping in your spare room. Lead the way," Tyson tells Jack, moving towards the staircase.

"No, Ms Claybourne gave you a single room. She asked me if you were bringing a guest, and I told her no, so she gave you and Claire single rooms," Jack replies, putting his foot right in it.

"Oh, I get it. You can't even sleep in a room near me. You're being so childish!" Claire shouts at Tyson. "How many times do I have to apologise? How long will you punish me for making a stupid mistake?"

"For as long as they chant Candy Cane Man at me at football games, I suppose," Tyson quips back angrily.

"It's fucking COTTON CANDY MAN!!"

~ Leila ~

Their temporary truce is so short lived that it almost gives me whiplash. Nate and Jack take Tyson to his room and tell me they will stock up the drink fridge in the games room. I frogmarch Claire into the kitchen and stare at her fiercely. Her bottom lip quivers for all of a second, before she inhales deeply and exhales. I know she's upset; I know she would take back everything that hurt Tyson if she could, but she can't.

"I think I should go," she tells me, her guard back up firmly in place. "My presence is obviously upsetting him, and I don't want to upset him anymore than I have." She looks around the room, eying up windows and doors for a means to escape.

Clicking my fingers in front of her to capture her full attention. "You're not going anywhere. I have to make Christmas dinner for everyone this evening, and if you bail on me now, they'll be eating raw turkey and carrots." She laughs a little, but I keep my expression stern. "You don't want to hurt him, but you keep shouting at him, Claire. He has every right to feel hurt. His sex life was plastered all over the national papers, the internet, social media."

"Don't you think I know that? We could have had something special, and I destroyed it before it even had a chance, Ley." Her voice breaks, causing her to stop. "There is just something about him that gets under my skin, and I lose my head. I will apologise to him properly once I've calmed down. I want to apologise for what I did because I never in a million years realised that stupid PDF could have the power to destroy another person. No, I'll rephrase that. That I could destroy someone, especially someone like Tyson."

Her head hangs in shame, and although Claire isn't usually a touchy-feely sort of person, I wrap my arms around her and hug her tight. "You never meant to hurt him; I know that. You made a mistake, and, in the process, you hurt yourself," I state, and when I hear her release a small cry, I want to cry with her.

As always, she wrecks the moment. "Gerroff me, you big girl. You'll have me weeping like an old maiden. What's done is done." That guard goes back up faster than I've ever seen. I swear to god, if we could bottle that and give it to goalkeepers and defenders, they would be impenetrable. "You can help me bring my stuff in then if I have to stay." She rolls her eyes and makes her way back to the front door.

Shortly after helping Claire, the gate alarm goes off again. This time Nate checks it and shouts to me after he does. "Hugo and Louise are here." With my other friend here, it feels like Christmas is finally underway. Hugo is a perfect gentleman, and although Claire rolls her eyes when he carries Louise's bag for her and kisses her hand, I know, deep down she is happy that Louise has found someone who treats her the way she wants to be treated.

While I show Louise and Hugo to their room, Claire sets up a station of festive drinks. When I return, she has arranged buck's fizz, mulled wine and eggnog in the entrance hall. She takes two glasses of buck's fizz and hands one to me. We clink glasses before drinking.

"I'm going to get busy in the kitchen for a while; I think you have more guests arriving," Claire tells me as the gate alarm beeps again. The last guests to arrive are Otis, one of Nate's friends, and his boyfriend, Liam. Otis is quite manly and gentlemanly while Liam is very flamboyant; he reminds me of a judge from a dancing show I used to watch.

"Darling, the place looks fabulous!" Liam proclaims with a waft of his full arm before air kissing me on both cheeks. "Where is that handsome man of yours?" he asks as he looks over my shoulder.

"I'm right here. Put my fiancée down, Liam, you'll make Otis jealous!" Otis' mouth twitches at the corners at Nate's joke.

"You mean he's making you jealous!" Otis quips back at Nate, causing him to laugh out loud.

Nate holds his hands up. "Guilty as charged! She's all mine!" he declares before pulling me to him. He's so good at playing the part. A little too good at times. It's easy to forget this is all a show when Nate is holding me in his arms like I'm his treasure.

After laughing with us, Otis reminds us they will be leaving tomorrow afternoon to visit his family down south. "We are so happy to be having Christmas dinner with you this evening, though; that was a lucky break!"

While Nate helps Otis and Liam to their room, I take the opportunity to take Missy for a little walk. Some fresh air and peace and quiet before the rest of the whirlwind is just what I need. Having made this walk several times a day since Nate gave me Missy, there is a well-worn path on the land that Nate owns. I'm about halfway around when I notice the tiny white flakes that float down majestically to the ground.

Our first Christmas, possibly our only Christmas together if we abide by the rules of our contract, is set to be a white one. I can't think of anything more perfect and poignant. It's so bittersweet that I want to run and tell Nate and drag him outside to see it for himself, and also cry, because there will never be another Christmas quite like this one.

This is a moment I want to freeze in time and never leave. A perfect, picturesque piece of flawlessness to commemorate my time with Nate.

Chapter 7

~ Nate ~

Once I escape Otis and Liam, I look for Leila. Claire is still in the kitchen and tells me Leila took Missy for a walk, so I pull on a jacket and follow her well-trodden path, hoping to catch up with her. I hear her before I see her. I have obviously been longer than I initially thought because she is already most of the way around the path, making her way back towards me. She doesn't notice me though. My girl is too busy dancing and laughing in the snowfall that has just begun.

As I watch her, my chest constricts. She is perfection. I'm in love with everything about her. This cannot be our only Christmas. I refuse to accept that. By the end of our contract, I want her to love me as much as I love her.

"Nate!" she calls out to me when she sees me. "It's snowing; it's going to be a white Christmas." She runs towards me with pure joy all over her face, so I open my arms to her. Her laugh rings out all around, and when she reaches me, I pick her up and spin us around. She throws her head back and spreads her arms, looking free and happy. Almost like a Christmas angel.

"I ordered the snow especially for you," I tell her. She has spoken so many times about how much she would love a white Christmas. It pained me that snow was the only thing money couldn't buy. She giggles before leaning down and kissing me.

"Oh, you did, did you?" she replies in between kisses.

"Yep. My girl wanted a white Christmas, and I want her to have everything her heart desires." In this tiny moment, I see the love and affection I have for Leila glowing back at me in her eyes. While we are both adults and aware that this is contractual right now, I don't doubt the depth of her feelings for me too. "Are you ready for Christmas mayhem, darling? Liam is getting ready as we speak, and Tyson is on his second or third beer. This could get messy."

"With you by my side, I'm ready for anything," she answers me as I lower her back to her feet. "So, what exactly is Liam's act?" she asks me curiously.

"He's a drag queen. When you see it, you'll understand. But basically, he becomes Camilla Chaos, a sassy southern diva who likes to sing and dance." I know that Leila is going to love this side of Liam. Although she doesn't know him well, we have spent time together as couples and I know she's very fond of him. "I wasn't sure at first, when Otis first started seeing him, but this is the happiest I have ever seen my friend." We hold hands as we crunch back up the pathway to the house.

"I can't wait!" Leila exclaims. Her cheeks and the tip of her nose are red from the cold. She looks adorable. As if on cue, music that must be coming from inside the house blurs loudly to us, and the deep dulcet tones of Camilla Chaos travel even further than the music.

"HEY, BIG SPENDER!" Camilla shouts, and our other guests can be heard laughing and singing along.

"Sounds like the party started without us, Nate," Leila shouts to me over the singing.

"We are the party! Come on, darling. This is what we've been looking forward to. Our own chosen family Christmas. I think we should do this every year from now on." The words fall out of my mouth before I can stop them.

"Nate! I-I. Look, let's not get too far ahead. We should enjoy what is right here, right now. You don't have to promise me anything beyond that," she tells me solemnly. Part of me wants to make her promise me we will do this every year, the desperate part that's frightened she'll walk away once the contract ends. Another part of me wants to shake her and tell her I am a grown man; I know my own mind and I know I love her and want every Christmas to be with her. Another part wants to scream at her for not feeling the same way I do, because if she did, wouldn't she just agree to what I am asking?

"That's what I want. I'm not going to change my mind or apologise for that. Now come on, I want to have a go at karaoke before Camilla sings Mariah Carey and breaks it again!" I'm glad that Leila allows the conversation to slide. I don't want to fight with her about this. I know it scares her. For some unknown reasons, she thinks I'm going to ditch her as soon as the clock ticks down on our contract. I just need to show her that I am claiming her as mine for always. I'll be swapping one contract for another; only this time, it'll be a marriage one and it'll be completely for real.

The smell of Christmas hits us as we walk inside. The food cooking, the mulled wine and the pine and orange scent from the fresh trees and wreath all mingle together to create the cosiest smell of Christmastime.

"Here they are, the love birds. We wondered where you'd got to," Jack calls out to us. Already I can see his cheeks are ruddy with his Christmas drink. Jack sits next to Tyson on the corner sofa, and the two friends laugh and giggle as Camilla sings out to them. Camilla loves to make people laugh, and this could be what is needed to break the ice between Tyson and Claire.

"I had to walk Missy. It has just started snowing!" Leila announces to everyone, and they all run to the windows to take a closer look.

"It's not sticking yet, but hopefully, in a couple more hours, there will be a lovely layer and we can build a snowman. Wouldn't that be nice, poppet?" Hugo laments to Louise, who looks at him awestruck. I've never seen a more perfect match. Well, except for Leila and I of course.

"Are you okay here, Nate? I'm going to help Claire in the kitchen." I kiss her in front of everyone, and I don't give two hoots when they holler, calling for us to get a room.

"I'll be waiting right here for you. Unless you want me to come and help?" I've barely finished the sentence when she shouts at me.

"No!"

Then to my utter astonishment, the whole lot of them shout at me.

"Nathan Cardal. Stay away from the kitchen!"

Well, so much for the season of goodwill!

"This song is dedicated to Mr Nathan Cardal, who has broken my heart by shacking up with the lovely Leila." Camilla laments to her audience, before breaking into Blue Christmas. Nate laughs hard at Camilla's pretend tears, while Otis shakes his head good naturedly.

"What other songs do you have?" Tyson asks us. I'm happy to see he's loosened up a little and isn't making the atmosphere tense. Maybe, just maybe everything is going to be okay. I should have known better.

Once Camilla has finished Blue Christmas, she takes a short break to freshen up and get a drink, and Tyson takes the opportunity to get up and sing. He chooses 'Last Christmas' by WHAM!. He sings it well, using humour at times, but I can't help but feel bad for Claire. Everyone in the room suspects that Tyson is singing about her. It seems he isn't through with embarrassing her.

Claire, however, barely looks at him. She continues to talk to Louis and Hugo as though nothing else could be happening right now. I am so proud of her for not rising to the bait.

Camilla takes the microphone back from Tyson and takes us on a journey of smooth crooners' Christmas songs. The mood is festive and mellow, and everyone seems to be happy.

An alarm sounds on Claire's iWatch, indicating it is time to check on the turkey, and so I follow her to the kitchen to help her. "I'll baste the turkey. Can you get the goose fat for the roast potatoes, please?" Claire says, taking charge in a way I've never seen before.

"Yeah, it's in the pantry. I'll only be a minute or two," I reply as I make my way to the storage room. The goose fat is on the shelf, exactly where Giovanni said it would be. I quickly pick up the two large jars and return to the kitchen. I can hear two voices inside when I get there, and not wanting to intrude, I wait outside.

"I didn't even think about the words until I was singing. I wouldn't do that, Claire. I hope you know that. I'm sorry if it seemed like it was directed at you." I realise Tyson is apologising to Claire and step away from the door. "I don't want an atmosphere or people walking on eggshells around us. Can we be friends? Please?"

"I'd like that. I am truly so sorry about everything, Tyson. I know you think I sold the story, but I didn't. However, I should never have said the things I did say. I was wrong." My heart swells with pride. They managed to sort it out all by themselves.

"I know. The media just blow everything up, and when you're in the eye of the storm, it can feel like the end of the world. Shake on it? Friends?" Tyson offers to her.

"Friends!" Claire confirms with a giggle. "Thank you. For coming to talk to me."

"Hey, what are friends for? The food smells lovely. Thank you for cooking. Come and have a drink with me later. I best get back to Jack." Knowing he is going to walk right at me, I pretend to be walking back from the pantry again.

His eyes widen when he sees me, like he's been caught doing something he shouldn't be. "Are you okay, Tyson? Are you looking for drinks?" I ask him innocently.

"Err, yeah. Drinks. They want more champagne." He covers, and so I walk back to the wine cooler and hand him two bottles. "Thanks, Doc," he says, making his way back to the rest of the gang.

Once he's out of earshot, I turn around to Claire with a massive grin on my face. "What was that all about, Ms Rippon?" I tease her good naturedly. She shocks me once again when she replies to me.

"No comment!" she says to me sternly. "Now, pass me that goose fat!"

My girl is learning!

~Nate ~

It's early evening and Leila, Claire and Louise are just about to serve us our Christmas dinner. My stomach growls at the delicious smells. I don't think I have ever looked forward to a Christmas dinner so much in all my life. In the past, my mother has hosted Christmas lunch on Christmas day, and a big meal at that time of the day has never appealed to me. This is much better. We decided that we would have our dinner on Christmas Eve so that we could eat with Otis and Liam. It also made more sense to eat a lighter fare on Christmas day because Jack and Tyson are playing the following day and Leila has to work too.

Leila and Claire have worked hard, and Louise too when she joined them towards the end. As the host, I ensure everyone has enough drinks and are seated comfortably. Hugo and Otis carry the starters through from the kitchen. There are a selection of different starters that we all tuck into enthusiastically. Leila sits beside me, her cheeks flushed from exertion, and eats her soup delicately, while I devour the king prawn cocktail. Hugo and Louise, the only vegetarians amongst us, feed each other melon balls. What sort of a starter is melon balls? I've never really understood it! It's more of a dessert than a starter for me.

Otis and Camilla clear away the starter dishes, Jack and I do another round of drinks and Tyson, under Leila's direction, distributes fresh cutlery and a Christmas cracker to every guest. With the help of Hugo, Otis and Camilla, the girls bring the feast to the table. Everything looks perfect and delicious, and I take pride that I had a hand in it all. I stayed away from the kitchen! Again, Hugo and Louise are given separate food that is suitable for vegetarians. Before I begin carving the turkey (Yes! They are allowing me to touch the food!) Leila stands up and clears her throat.

"A-hem. I won't keep you long, I promise. I know we are all eager to eat our lovely Christmas dinner. I just wanted to thank you all for being here today and for being our chosen family. We couldn't have chosen better." Everyone raises their glasses to Leila in toast. "I would also like to thank Claire for making this dinner possible. It is thanks to her that we are still having this amazing feast today, and I think she deserves a round of applause."

We all break out into grateful clapping; I smile when I observe Tyson leaning over to thank Claire, and I nod to her appreciatively when I cut into the golden skin on the turkey to reveal juicy white meat. Once I've cut enough meat for us all, I sit next to Leila, who brandishes her Christmas cracker at me. We pull it until it rips apart, making its trademark snap when it does. As always there is a joke and a paper crown inside that I push onto her head. We repeat the process with my cracker, and I also pull on my paper hat.

Our chosen family all follow suit, even Camilla, who complains about how long she curled her hair for and now it'll be flattened because of the paper hat. We all look ridiculous. It's hilarious. This is what families should be doing. Spending time together, having simple, good-hearted fun and a warm meal together.

"There used to be little plastic toys in the crackers when I was little. What happened to them?" Tyson asks, looking inside his cracker to see if he missed something.

"Yeah, I remember them. My dad got a plastic bat once, but he thought it was a fake moustache. He even attached it to his nose." We all laugh in reply, nodding in recognition and retelling our own stories of years gone by.

"Well, these ones are environmentally friendly. Everything is recyclable. We are trying to do our bit for the sea turtles," Leila tells our guests. I did offer to buy the more luxurious crackers that had items of jewellery inside. However, Leila said that everyone eating at our table has more than enough wealth and frivolity and she asked if we could make a donation to the local food bank instead, which we did.

We are all too stuffed after dinner to eat dessert, so we opt to have that later this evening. Jack, Tyson and I are responsible for clearing up and loading the dishwashers. This is the only time I will be allowed in the kitchen.

"We need to do this every year, Nathan. This is the best Christmas we've ever had," Jack says to me, even as he scrapes plates and loads them into the dishwasher. A twinge of panic twists inside me. I want to promise him and everyone else that our home will always be open for Christmas. However, I don't want to do that if it's without Leila. She is Christmas for me now. She is my whole world, and it would be too painful to try and recreate this if she doesn't stick around. "Go on, go back to your girl. We've got this, right, Tyson?" Tyson smiles at me; I think he is more than a little merry from all the beer and champagne.

I wink at my brother and thank him. "I'll see you both in a minute." And head back to find Leila.

"She's just gone to freshen up," Claire tells me when I walk into the lounge, so I take the opportunity to find Leila and spend a few minutes alone with her.

"Nate? Is that you?" Leila calls out when I open the bedroom door.

"Yes!" I assure her.

"Oh good. I can give you a glimpse of one of your Christmas presents." She steps out of her dressing room, dressed as a slutty Santa. With a little fur edged red velvet dress and a Santa hat perched on her head, she looks good enough to eat.

"I haven't had my dessert yet," I tell her, licking my lips.

"I am your dessert."

~ Leila ~

Just as I hoped he would, Nate follows me up to our bedroom. Everyone else is having a break after our lovely dinner, so I thought now would be the ideal time to slip off and give Nate one of my surprises all for him.

He bought us some toys, but I invested in some dress up. Tonight, I am his slutty Santa. The dress is a little tight and probably too short for what would be considered decent, but seeing as decent is a long way from what I am offering, it seems the perfect size.

After telling him that I am his dessert, he stands staring at me with his mouth open in what I hope is a happy surprise. My body is already humming with need. It seems such a long time since our session last night, and I am eager for more. Will I ever get enough of him? I doubt it. I crave him and his touch more than ever. I don't think that will ever stop.

"You look so fucking hot. I love the dress, but I also want to rip you open like a Christmas present. I am so confused!" I giggle with him, happy that he likes my dress; his praise sends zings of pleasure to my pussy, causing it to ache with need.

"I am wearing it for you. What you do with me now is completely up to you," I tell him as I push him to sit on the edge of the bed. I gently sway my hips and move my body seductively in front of him.

"Okay, I want to fuck you while you're wearing it, but I don't want to ruin it. I want to keep it so you can wear it for me again next year," he confesses to me as he drags me closer to him.

"This isn't machine washable; you'll have to be very careful." I warn him. I probably shouldn't warn him; it'll only encourage him to not be careful if experience is anything to go off.

"Fuck it, I'll buy you another one." I kneel up on the ground in front of him and unzip his pants. His cock is already hard and struggling to be free. "You have no idea how much I want you right now. How much I need to bury myself deep inside you and feel you coming around my cock. I can't get enough of you."

With a gentle slap against his stomach, his cock is finally free. "Hmmm." I hum while I swirl my tongue around the tip, smiling internally when he groans. I lick all the way down his shaft, along the taut skin and down to his balls, which I pepper with soft kisses. Then I retrace my path back up to the head of his glorious cock. I wrap my lips around it, opening my jaw as far as I can so I can take as much of him in my mouth as possible. Nate moans out and threads his fingers through my hair, holding my head in place while I suck him. I stroke his cock with my tongue and mouth, hollowing out my cheeks and slurping. His cock pulses in reaction, while Nate gasps and revels in the sensations. When he hits the back of my throat, I quicken my pace, knowing he loves it. I roll his balls in my hand, while holding his dick in place with the other. His reactions and knowing that I have the power to make him forget himself completely and utterly turn me on so much. The ache in my tummy is constant as my need for him grows with each suck, each lick, and with every caress.

"Baby! Baby, stop. Stop!" he whispers to me, pulling away from my mouth. "I need to fuck you; I haven't even touched you yet."

"Just let me take care of you then," I offer. Nate often gets me off and asks for nothing in return. In fact, he is generous to a fault. Even though I am wound up tightly and desperate for his touch, I would forgo my pleasure to give him his.

"Nah, baby, you don't get it. Getting you off is my pleasure. It's my drug. I'm addicted to you. I just need you." He lifts me from the floor and tears my dress from me. "I owe you a dress. You are the best present I've ever unwrapped."

"Yeah, you do; I'll send you the bill. Take my thong off; you can owe me for that too," I tell him with a giggle. It is only a cheap dress up, nothing to worry about. "Where do you want me?"

"Bend over for me. Can I use a toy too, darling. I want you to take all of me inside you and try the toy too, if that's okay?" I crouch on all fours on the floor. The need for him is now too much.

"Nate? Please!" I plead with him. The cool air hits my pussy as I arch my back impatiently. When his warm mouth eats me out from behind, my arms almost give way.

"Oh, baby, you taste delicious. You are so wet. You need me, don't you?" His fingers take over from where his tongue left off before he turns on the toy he wants to use. It's a small vibe, which hums away as Nate presses it against my clit. My legs begin to shake as the pleasure builds into a crescendo. I arch my back even more when I feel his cock pressing against me. "You're more than ready for me, aren't you, Leila?"

"Yes, I want you now, Nate. I need you."

"You're so fucking sexy when you beg me to fuck you." And with one swift thrust, he pushes fully inside me.

"Again!" I shout; that was too delightful to only do once. He withdraws fully from me, slaps my ass and then thrusts into me once again, hitting my g-spot, spreading my inner walls wide while he moves with deep strokes inside me. A finger against my back hole pushes me over the cliff's edge. "Nate!" I call as my body contracts and contorts almost involuntarily. It's so powerful that my arms give out. Nate holds me up by my hips and thrusts another couple of times before finishing deep inside me too.

"Oh, my days, that was good!" I tell him when my breathing returns to a more normal rate. "Merry Christmas, handsome." He chuckles as he withdraws from me, handing me a towel to clean up with.

"It's been like Christmas every day since we met. I have a lot to be thankful for," he says to me almost bashfully. "I never want this to end, Leila."

While he's feeling sentimental, I push his Christmas PJ's into his hands. "You'll wear your Christmas jimjams like me, then?" I ask him sweetly, giving him my puppy dog eyes.

He chuckles in reply. "Okay, okay. If it'll make you happy, I'll wear the jimjams, but you have to defend my honour if the others make fun of me."

"Always. I will always have your back." I sincerely mean that. Even beyond our fake engagement and forced cohabitation. You can't share a Christmas with someone the way Nate and I have and go back to being strangers. Nate will always be a massive part of me. I guess he just gave me another Christmas present.

Christmas Crackers
(NOUN)

A tube of brightly coloured paper, usually given at Christmas parties, that makes a noise (snap) when pulled apart by two people. They usually contains small presents, paper hats and jokes/trivia.

(SOURCE: Cambridge Dictionary)

Chapter 9

~ Nate ~

With a final push inside her, I come while Leila contracts around me. Stars blind my vision and my heart slams against my chest as euphoria courses through my body. I'm reluctant to leave her, but we've already been away from our guests for longer than we should have.

Her Santa dress lays torn on the ground. I should feel bad, but I have no regrets. Getting to tear her open like my very own Christmas present will probably be my favourite gift this year, and I will order another dress for her asap. I can't help but relent when she asks me to wear the god-damn Christmas PJs she bought me. They match hers perfectly, and if I am completely honest, they are quite comfortable. I won't let Leila know that though.

I am relieved when we return to the lounge and find everyone apart from Otis and Camilla in their Christmas PJs too. Even Jack has a Nordic Christmas onesie and matching Christmas socks. Leila really has gone all out, and everyone is enjoying the festive touches she has put so much thought into.

Jack and Tyson play on the games console, while Camilla ramps things up with some upbeat Christmas songs. Hugo comes to sit by me when Louise prises herself away from him to sit with her best friends. They play cards and board games and enjoy drinks together

"Thank you for inviting us all here, Nate. Louise is in heaven!" Otis tells me. "I'm having the best time," he continues, and I jovially slap him on the shoulder. I bet there will be wedding bells in the near future for him. He seems to be as hooked on Louise as I am on Leila.

"It seems we have both found someone special. How cool is it that they are best friends, and we are too," I say to him. In an ideal world, we could double date and our children could grow to also be best friends.

"I've never met anyone like Louise before. Meeting her has completely changed everything. I'm so glad you and Leila fell in love and are now getting married, or all this might not be happening," he confides in me with a hushed whisper.

We toast to our ladies, and a tiny twinge of guilt at deceiving one of my oldest friends threatens to raise its ugly head, but I fight it down. I'm sure that, somewhere along the line, Leila and I were meant to meet and be together. We are made the same, want the same. We were made for each other. I have no doubt about it. She belongs with me, and I to her. Spending our first Christmas together confirms that I want to spend every holiday and special occasion with her. There is no one else that could compare.

Leila directs us to the theatre that has also been decorated festively. "We are going to watch a Christmas film." I sit next to my love and share the fresh popcorn that has been left in my armrest. Leila rests her head on my shoulder, and I wrap my arm around her. "This has all been perfect, darling. Thank you for everything you have done for us all."

"This is the best Christmas ever. This is everything I've ever wanted. All we need now is to check the sky for Santa, and hopefully, there will be enough snow to build a snowman." I kiss her temple, wanting more than ever for her to have the white Christmas she deserves.

When the movie finishes, I tell everyone we will be going outside to look for Santa and to check if the snow has stuck. Claire, Jack and Tyson come with us, but the others wave us off, telling us they are too comfortable and outside is far too dark and cold.

Before we go out, I insist that Leila wraps. She insists that everyone else has to wrap up too. By the time we pass over the threshold, we are all bundled up like snowmen. The snow is still thin on the ground, but it continues to fall in a light flurry. When a light appears in the sky, Leila squeals in delight that it must be Rudolph's nose. Jack and Tyson, unable to resist, make tiny snowballs and start a mini war between us. We may not have enough snow to make a snowman, but we can still have a lot of fun. Leila and Claire team up against us, and it's not long before we have them surrounded and bombard them with the smallest snowballs known to man.

"We concede, we give up! You win!" Leila calls to us, and I waste no time in returning to her. I pick her up in a fireman's lift over my shoulder to her screeches of outrage. "Put me down, Nate!"

"No, you conceded, and now you're all mine," I shout back to her as I run towards the front door.

"Put me down or I won't give you the rest of your Christmas presents!" She threatens me. I quickly place her on her feet at the front door.

"Hey, you've already given him some of his presents? That's not fair! What about me?" Jack calls out from behind us.

Even though he doesn't know what my present was, I still glare at him. I don't share. Especially not Leila. "It was a special present that only I can have. All mine!"

"Gross!" he replies, forgetting that he was the one who showed an initial interest in her.

"Nah, fucking amazing is what it was," I add, earning a pinch off Leila and a fake puking face off Jack. After checking my watch for the time, I tell Jack, "It's after midnight; you can open your own presents now."

There is a collective whoop, and it's even better when we open the front door and the smell of hot cocoa hits us all. Hugo and Louise bring out hot chocolate with cream and marshmallows for us all, which we take back to the biggest tree in the lounge, where all the presents are nestled under the tree.

I sit back with Leila and watch as the others light up with joy when they open their gifts. "Nate, I want to give you the gifts I picked for you, but after you bought me a car, it doesn't feel like anywhere near enough," she tells me bashfully. "I went down the sentimental route. I will get you something else soon."

"Darling, anything you give me is more than enough. The fact that you've put time and thought into a gift for me means more than money ever could. Please show me."

She lifts up a medium sized box that is wrapped in a large red bow and places it on my lap. "Merry Christmas, Nate. I made you this box so that if you're so inclined, you'll always have a way to remember our time together this season."

The bow falls away almost fluidly, and my heart rate increases in anticipation. Inside, there is a collection of items: a menu from the restaurant at the docks, from our first official date; a keyring of the Eiffel Tower; the magazine spread we did to announce our engagement; Missy's first collar; her football shirt with 'Future Mrs Nate Cardal' emblazoned on the back; a pad and pencil from the Peninsula Rooftop suite that we stayed in in Paris, the place we first slept together.

The final item is a traditional photo album. It has all her photos from the past few months, a couple of me sleeping, loads of us together and a couple of me and Missy that I didn't know she had taken. At around halfway, there is writing on the page.

> *Nate,*
> *The past few months have been the best of my life.*
> *Thank you for sharing them with me.*
> *There is plenty of space to document even more memories.*
> *Love always,*
> *Leila x*

For the first time in my life, I am rendered speechless. There is so much I want to say, and yet none of it will ever be enough to convey to this woman exactly how much she means to me. "I told you it's nothing much, just sentimental–"

Before she can finish, I kiss her. A possessive, grateful, completely filled with love type of kiss. When I pull away, she looks dazed. "This is the best present anyone has ever given me. I love it. I love every single bit of it. And I love you," I tell her, even though I know I shouldn't. I forget everything and everyone around us. All that matters is Leila and me.

The rest of our guests upon seeing my display of affection catcall us, but I could not care less.

"I love you too, Nate. Merry Christmas."

"Merry Christmas, darling."

"Oh, I almost forgot. I have one more gift for you." Leila passes an envelope to me, which I open. She begins to giggle as I read the contents.

"Cookery classes?" I shout, and everyone bursts into laughter. The minx bought me cookery classes!

We have another couple of drinks as we wind down. Just before we go to bed, I notice Tyson following Claire when she says goodnight. Maybe all is not lost there. I know it would make Leila happy if they were able to move on together.

All in all, our Substitution Christmas has been the best Christmas ever.

~ Jack ~

Even though I am alone, this Christmas turned out to be a lot better than I thought it would. I hope next year I have someone special to share it with too. It's only when I see Tyson run after Claire at bedtime that I realise how lonely I really feel. All around me are happy couples, and it's great. However, the hole in my life seems to get bigger by the second.

Christmas day morning arrives, and before I go down to help with breakfast, I wash and dress. Leila and Nathan have requested that we go to church today, and I promised that I would. It should be a laugh with Tyson too.

I'm greeted by Claire at Tyson's bedroom door. She looks embarrassed, but I just ask if he is awake yet, hoping to put her at ease.

"Actually, Jack, he's gone home. I tried to call him, but he blocked me." Her embarrassment makes more sense now, and I have to be honest and admit that my friend's actions have shocked and appalled me. I have treated some girls callously in the past, but this takes the biscuit!

"He's an asshole. He shouldn't have treated you like that. Don't let his ego stop you from enjoying Christmas." She doesn't look convinced, so I divulge more information. "I need your help. Nathan and Leila are making us go to church today. I might combust if I walk into the church or die of boredom. I need you to be my wing woman, and I'll be your wingman."

She smiles at me, a genuine smile, and nods her agreement. "Thanks, Jack. I feel so humiliated that I was considering going back to my dad's house. But if you need my help, I'll stay a little longer." And true to her word, she does. She attends the church service with us all and helps Leila prepare the buffet food. However, when Otis and Liam make their departure, she does too, under the guise of not wanting her father to be alone on Christmas.

On boxing day morning, we set out early for the training centre. We will play All Saints at 2 pm and it's important for us to train and warm up properly. When I arrive at the gym, Tyson is already here, and he looks terrible.

"What the fuck, man?" I say to him, shaking my head. "Why did you leave like that? I thought you and Claire had made up?"

"It was a mistake. I should never have opened that can of worms again." He sits next to his locker with his head in his hands. "I thought I would be okay with everything, but I woke up next to her and I was scared. She destroyed me last time, and I'm still not over it. I don't think I'll ever move past it."

"She seemed pretty cut up about it. She went home too," I tell him, because I think he ought to know that his actions hurt people too. "I do think she genuinely regrets the whole list thing."

"I'm not denying it. I wish I could change how I feel, but I can't. Just because she's sorry doesn't mean I can move past what happened. I'm still pretty mad at her. I thought she was special. I thought I was special to her. But it was all a con," he retorts bitterly.

"You should at least talk to her. Clear the air once and for all," I offer, sitting next to him on the bench. "I didn't realise you liked her that much."

"The moment I saw her, I felt a connection to her. But, I had it all wrong. I'm a fucking idiot. She'll be selling the story as we speak, making a mockery of me again," he assures me. "I've blocked her everywhere, and I'm just going to keep my head down and maintain a distance from her. Hopefully, next year Nathan and Leila will be abroad or pregnant and won't want a substitute family for Christmas."

No matter how much I believe he is wrong, Tyson's hurt and humiliation is still too raw to let him see past the bad stuff that happened. The best thing I can do is let it drop and support my friend. His game form has suffered recently, and I know the chants and speculations about him are responsible for that. I can't even imagine how I'd feel if I thought I found someone special and she hurt me in such a public manner.

"Fuck all that anyway. The important thing is that we win this game today! It would put us at the top of the table." He smiles and nods. Brothers in arms once again.

Playing football in winter is always exhilarating. We play in shorts, and it's snowing. Sweat covers my body, and yet the air I breathe in stings and appears as fluffy clouds when I exhale. The crowd, as always, is amazing. Up in the stands with their hats and scarves and cups of hot tea to ward off the cold, they show true dedication to both the team and the club. I want to make them proud; they deserve this.

After a tense start, our opponents begin to make mistakes, and we take advantage of it. Tyson bags the first goal. A screamer of a header that only a powerhouse like him could manage. I run to celebrate with him and even do the stupid dance from a video game we play in front of the cameras.

In the second half, I score a spectacular goal from a free kick, causing our fans to explode in excitement. They chant my name and sing my song; it doesn't get any better than this. I run to the corner where a lot of our fans are to celebrate to a chorus of 'Jack's our Lad'. And right before full time, I manage to score one last goal from a corner.

Lionhearts music rings out over the speakers as we celebrate as a team and club and await the final whistle to indicate the end of the game.

Sports News Channel request a post-match interview with me and present me with the Man of the Match trophy. Live on air, they ask what charity I wish to donate the prize of £10,000 to.

"The local children's hospital. I made some amazing friends there a few days ago, and they deserve your love and support more than ever." I didn't think anything could make me happier than football could, but as a warm feeling spreads to my chest, I know I've found something that will fulfil me more than anything. Helping others.

It is tradition to celebrate Christmas with the team after the match and this year is no exception. The glaring difference this year is that Nathan sticks around and spends most of his time with Leila. Maybe, no *hopefully,* next year, that'll be me.

> Merry Christmas. Love, Jack, Nathan, Leila, Tyson, Claire, Louise, Hugo, Otis, Liam/Camilla and Missy xxx

Emma Lee-Johnson

A happily married mum of three, originally from Liverpool, UK. Now a self-published author of Paranormal, Contemporary and Mafia romances that are hot and sweet!

I am a hopeless romantic, with a gutter mind and a potty mouth, but I promise my heart is pure gold!

Books by this Author include:

- The Alpha's Property
- The Alpha's Heir
- Festive Flings
- More Than Just a Fling
- Festive Wedding
- The Hidden Queen of Alphas
- Substitution Clause

Emma Lee-Johnson

Romance Author

https://viewauthor.at/emmaleejohnson

instagram.com/author_emma_lee

tiktok.com/@emmaleejohnson

facebook.com/profile.php?id=100064632064511

Follow me on social media for exclusive content and updates.

Amazon: viewauthor.at/emmaleejohnson

Facebook Page: Emma Lee-Johnson
Facebook group: Emma's Angels with Attitude

facebook.com/groups/656345582368378
Instagram author_emma_lee
TikTok.com/@emmaleejohnson
Goodreads Emma Lee-Johnson
Ko-fi.com/emmaleejohnson
Emmalee-johnson.com
linktr.ee/emmaleejohnson

If you have enjoyed reading More Than Just a Fling, please leave a review.

Thank you for reading!

AN ENGLISH ELITE FOOTBALL LEAGUE ROMANCE

SUBSTITUTION
Clause

EMMA LEE-JOHNSON

Leila Monrose has a life many would envy. In her prestigious career as an injury specialist in Elite English Football, she meets interesting people and travels the world. Beautiful and clever, she has a nice car, a stylish home and has made plenty of friends since she moved up north for her job. Sooner or later, someone will come along to share it all with her.

Could it be the younger footballer, Jack Cardal, who Leila helped regain form after a nasty injury? Handsome, rich and confident, Jack always wants what he can't have. When Leila declines his invitation to dinner, he sees it as a challenge.

Or maybe it will be his older brother, billionaire property and technology tycoon-turned-football club investor Nate Cardal, who is a perfect gentleman with a massive skeleton in his closet.

When one brother hurts her, the other helps her seek revenge, but with conditions attached.

In a world of high-stakes contracts, will Leila activate the Substitution Clause?

Available NOW: mybook.to/SubstitutionClause

FESTIVE FLINGS

Set in the festive weeks before Christmas and New Year, Festive Flings follows the intertwining romantic lives of 6 people at different stages in their lives and sexual experiences.

Recently dumped Jamie is ready to move on in time for the holidays, unaware that her boss has been secretly pining over her. Their colleague, Tim, meets the woman of his dreams, but her nightmare of a family has left her self-confidence in tatters. And Jamie's sister, Billie, is hoping for a Christmas miracle to rekindle the passion in her marriage, where kink has been replaced with kids.

Fun, fetishes and frolicking combine in an intertwining tale of spicy British romance in the weeks leading up to Christmas.

All you need for Christmas is... a festive fling!

This book is extremely hot and should be read with caution! Reported side effects reported include: involuntary Kegel and spontaneous pantie-wetting incidents. Read at your own risk... And pleasure!

Available now on Amazon

Acknowledgments

Football plays a massive part in our family, and Christmas is no exception. My husband says Liverpool FC is his religion, and he's not far from the truth in that statement. He lives and breathes LFC and loves the club almost as much as he loves me (he promises me he loves me more, but I can't be 100% sure lol). Football and in particular Liverpool Football Club will always be in my heart, because it is the heart of my love. Cut him and he'll bleed Liverpool Red. And now, our boys share that love too. It's more than a football club, Anfield is our church and Klopp and the boys are our idols. So there you go, there are my muses for this series.

To my best friend and soul mate, I love you all the world, and also our three boys SCJ, I'm so proud to be your mum.

To the friends who have never stopped supporting me. Thank you from the bottom of my heart. This authoring business is a lot tougher than anyone can realise and without the support of my friends, I would have given in by now. With special shout outs for Melody and Mariarosa for the support and sprints, Katie Gwilt of Katie Gwilt Creations for all the merch and cocks, and to Aimee of Book Babes UK, for showcasing my first Christmas Romance book: Festive Flings in her Book Boxes (Available on a monthly basis from her website: https://bookbabesuk.shop/)

As always, to my amazing editor, Steph. Thank you for attempting to teach me, and for catching all the comma's I misplace/forget. You are a star.

Printed in Great Britain
by Amazon